Don't Worry, Croc!

An Ivy and Mack story

Written by Rebecca Colby

Illustrated by Gustavo Mazali

Collins

Who's in this story?

Listen and say

Mum

Miss Sweet

Alex

Mack

Download the audio at www.collins.co.uk/839720

Ivy

CLASS 3

Mack says, "I don't want to go to school."

Ivy says, "I love school."

Mack says, "I love home school with Croc."

Mack says, "Can Croc come to school, Mum?"

Mum says, "Yes, Mack."

Mack says, "Croc doesn't like
the classroom."

Ivy says, "Look, there's your teacher, Miss Sweet. She's very nice."

CLASS 1

Miss Sweet says, "Hello, Mack!"

Mack says, "Please don't go!"
Ivy says, "Don't worry. You have got Croc."

Miss Sweet says, "Here is your book. Have you got a pencil?"

Mack says, "This is Croc. Croc has got his pencil case."

Mack says, "I don't know the alphabet. But I can write my name!"

Miss Sweet says, "Don't worry.
This is Alex."

Alex says, "Sit with me."

Alex and Mack write.

Mack says, "Don't worry, Croc. Write with me."

Alex and Mack draw.

Mack says, "Don't worry, Croc.
Draw with me."

Alex and Mack play.

Mack says, "Don't worry, Croc.
Play with me."

Ivy says, "Do you and Croc like school?"

Mack says, "Croc isn't coming to school today."

Ivy says, "Doesn't Croc like school?"

Mack says, "I like our school but Croc likes home school."

Have a nice day, Mack.

Picture dictionary

Listen and repeat

alphabet	book

classroom

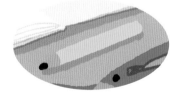
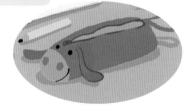

pencil	pencil case

1 Look and order the story

2 Listen and say

Collins

Published by Collins
An imprint of HarperCollins*Publishers*
Westerhill Road
Bishopbriggs
Glasgow
G64 2QT

HarperCollins*Publishers*
1st Floor, Watermarque Building
Ringsend Road
Dublin 4
Ireland

William Collins' dream of knowledge for all began with the publication of his first book in 1819.

A self-educated mill worker, he not only enriched millions of lives, but also founded a flourishing publishing house. Today, staying true to this spirit, Collins books are packed with inspiration, innovation and practical expertise. They place you at the centre of a world of possibility and give you exactly what you need to explore it.

10 9 8 7 6 5 4 3 2

ISBN 978-0-00-839720-3

Collins® and COBUILD® are registered trademarks of HarperCollins*Publishers* Limited

www.collins.co.uk/elt

British Library Cataloguing in Publication Data

A catalogue record for this publication is available from the British Library.

Author: Rebecca Colby
Illustrator: Gustavo Mazali (Beehive)
Series editor: Rebecca Adlard
Publishing manager: Lisa Todd
Product managers: Jennifer Hall and Caroline Green
In-house editor: Alma Puts Keren
Project manager: Emily Hooton
Editor: Deborah Friedland
Proofreaders: Natalie Murray and Michael Lamb
Cover designer: Kevin Robbins
Typesetter: 2Hoots Publishing Services Ltd
Audio produced by id audio, London
Reading guide author: Julie Penn
Production controller: Rachel Weaver
Printed and bound by: GPS Group, Slovenia

MIX
Paper from
responsible sources
FSC C007454
www.fsc.org

This book is produced from independently certified FSC™ paper to ensure responsible forest management.

For more information visit: **www.harpercollins.co.uk/green**

Download the audio for this book and a reading guide for parents and teachers at www.collins.co.uk/839720